igloo

igloo

Published in 2008
by Igloo Books Ltd
Cottage Farm,
Sywell,
NN6 0BJ
www.igloo-books.com

10 9 8 7 6 5 4 3 2 1

ISBN: 978 1 84561 932 9

Cover design by Insight Design
Cover illustrated by © Rachel Ellen Designs Ltd
Interior illustrations by Liz and Kate Pope

Printed and manufactured in China

The Mystery
of the
Mixed-up Disco

by Carol Lawrence

igloo

Chapter 1

The Announcement

Poppy couldn't wait to phone her best friend, KC, with the news. KC had left school early to go to the dentist, so she hadn't heard the head teacher, Mrs. Clarke, making an announcement about the disco. Poppy was fidgeting impatiently as she waited for KC to come to the phone; she seemed to take ages.

"Hi there," said KC at last.

"Guess what?" gasped Poppy, excitedly. "There's going to be a disco at school next Friday. Everyone over the age of eight can enter. And better still – there's going to be a dance competition. And, even better – and best of all – the winner will be on TV!"

Poppy could hardly contain herself. KC was as excited as she was and wanted to hear all about it. It would be their first school disco. Poppy told her everything Mrs. Clarke had told them.

"The producer of a new show for children's TV

is coming to the disco, and she'll be looking out for the best dancer to give them a part. We can all prepare a dance routine and pick a song to dance to, and dance, just on our own, for her to see how good we are!"

It wasn't just going to be a brilliant night out; it could even make someone – someone in their school – a star!

"I can't wait," Poppy shouted excitedly. It was so loud KC had to move the phone away from her ear. "It will be so much fun. You've got to come. Everyone is coming."

"I'll be far too scared to do a dance on my own," KC confided. "Can we do a dance together? Please? I won't be so scared if we're with each other."

Poppy smiled to herself. She was scared of

dancing on her own, too – and KC knew it. They planned to meet up the next day, which luckily was Saturday. They would work out what they could wear, start practising dance moves and choose their music. Poppy felt she would burst with excitement.

On Saturday morning, Poppy ate her breakfast as quickly as she could so that she could rush off to KC's house.

"Can I come?" asked Sam, her seven-and-a-half-year old brother. Poppy sighed. She knew Sam would soon get impatient with them talking about clothes and wanting to work out dance moves. But if he was at home on his own with mum and dad, they'd make him tidy his room and brush his hair, which were both things Sam hated more than anything – even more than watching nine-year-old girls try on clothes and practise dances.

"You can," Poppy said at last. "As long as you promise not to complain, and to help us do some research into the TV show."

"Yes, sir!" said Sam, and Poppy laughed. Sam

was always happy to use the computer to do some research. He could find things out twice as quickly as anyone else she knew. And he loved being able to show Poppy and KC how good at it he was – it easily made up for being the youngest.

When they got to KC's house, KC's mum was reading the paper, but KC was in her room with absolutely all of her clothes spread all over the bed, the chair and the floor.

"What do you think of this one?" she asked holding up a sparkly top as they squeezed through the door – it wouldn't open very far because of the huge pile of t-shirts squashed behind it. "Do you think it goes with these glittery tights?" she asked Poppy.

Sam made a face, and Poppy nudged him in the ribs.

"I told you, you have to be good," she hissed. But KC laughed.

"Poor Sam," she said. "He's not going to have a good morning. Unless you want to try on some of these?" She held up some old bright yellow leggings. Sam's eyebrows came together over his nose, like caterpillars squaring up for a fight. Before he had a chance to answer, Poppy came to his rescue.

"I said he could do some research on the computer", she said. "To find out more about the TV series."

KC showed Sam to her mother's home office. Her mum had given them permission to use the computer.

As soon as Sam was out of the way, Poppy and KC set about the serious business of sorting through all of KC's clothes to find something she could wear to the disco. They found the perfect skirt, t-shirt and tights and even found some sparkly shoes.

"You look so good in pink and purple," said Poppy enviously. "Although everything looks good on you."

"But you could wear these!" said KC, tossing her some jeans with a glittery patch. Poppy laughed and her bright green eyes sparkled. She started trying on KC's clothes. Luckily, they were both about the same size.

All too soon, it was lunchtime, and Sam dashed in.

"I've found out loads," he said. "The series is called 'The Towers of Moffat Island'. It's about a school in an old castle on an island –"

"Don't tell me – let me guess – called Moffat Island!" laughed Poppy.

"And the kids at the school think it's too boring there so they start doing exciting things. Like they start a band and they have late night discos and –"

"Don't they have to go home at night?" asked KC.

"No, it's a boring school."

"I think you mean a boarding school," said

Poppy.

"Whatever," said Sam.

"It's not Sam's fault," said KC. "Tell us more, Sam."

"There'll be eight shows to start with and, if it's good, they'll make more. The person who wins the disco competition will be in three shows. There's a trailer you can watch on the website. Do you want to see it?"

They all sat and watched the trailer, eating sandwiches that KC's mum brought up for them.

The trailer for the show looked really great. The castle was really spooky and had lots of spiky towers.

"We just have to be in that!" breathed KC. "It would be so cool! Let's work on some dance moves. Sam – could you find us some good dance music on the computer, please? Poppy and I need to practice!"

Leaving the rest of their sandwiches on their plates, the two girls started dancing around to the music Sam found. They whirled and bounced around the room, until KC's mum came to see why they were making so much noise.

"I think you should practice downstairs," she said. "At this rate, you'll bring the ceiling down! Sam, are you going to enter the dance competition?"

Sam looked surprised.

"It doesn't say it has to be a girl," said KC. "I think you should at least try." Sam looked scared – he turned to Poppy, hoping she would help him out. He didn't want to have to dance. He hated dancing.

"He's too young," Poppy said. Sam breathed a sigh of relief. "Remember, all the other characters in the series are nine or ten. But Sam can help us to choose the music. He's such a whiz on the computer and he'll be able to find us a great dance track."

The girls spent the rest of the afternoon working out dance moves, while Sam found lots of great songs from new bands for them to dance to. He really was the best at finding stuff on the Internet. By four o'clock, when it was time to go home, they'd chosen a perfect track that no one else would have heard. Sam wrote down the web address so that Poppy could practice at home. She couldn't wait to carry on dancing!

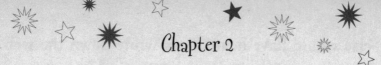

Chapter 2

A New Dancer

At school on Monday, everyone was talking about the disco. In the playground, all the girls were bouncing around, kicking their legs out, waving their arms around and trying out complicated dance moves they'd seen on television. Some fell over, or crashed into each other and started giggling. The girls who did ballet class on Saturday were much better at it than the others.

"Look at that girl, there," Poppy said to KC. "She's really good. Who is she?"

KC turned to see to where Poppy was pointing.

"She's a new girl. She's only just started at the school. She's in Mrs. Dean's class, I think. Her name is Paulina. She really is good, isn't she? Almost as good as Shantaê."

"Oh, I'd forgotten about Shantaê!" Poppy said. "She's bound to win! Where is she?"

Their classmate wasn't anywhere in the playground.

"I don't think she's in school today," said KC.

"I hope she's better in time for the disco on Friday", Poppy said. "She's by far the best dancer in the school. Even that new girl won't be able to beat her!"

Poppy and KC settled to watching Paulina until the bell went for the next lesson. It was sports. Mrs. Dean's class was doing sports, too. They were in the gym and Poppy and KC were supposed to be playing netball. But as soon as they had got changed, Mrs. Clarke called them all into the gym.

"Today, you can do disco-dancing instead of netball – to get you in the mood for Friday!"

Mrs. Clarke smiled and turned on the CD player. She had brought along a CD of disco music and they all danced as energetically as they could for the whole lesson. Mrs. Clarke went around the room watching everyone and making suggestions to some of the girls.

At the end of the lesson, they were all out of breath and red in the face. They flopped down on the floor while Mrs. Clarke spoke to the two classes.

"Look at you, you're all exhausted! That shows that dancing is really good exercise for you," she said. "Paulina, your dancing is very good. Do you go to dance lessons? And where's Shantaê today?"

Paulina looked pleased.

"I used to go to a jazz ballet class before I moved," she said. "But I haven't got a dance class here yet. I've only been here a couple of weeks."

"Well, when Shantaê's back in school you can ask her where she has lessons. She goes to several classes, I think. Her mother used to be a dancer."

They all trooped out of the gym to the changing rooms. Paulina was trailing behind, looking at the notices on the wall.

"Hi," said Poppy. "I'm Poppy and this is KC. You're very good at dancing. Are you going to be in the competition?"

"I don't know," Paulina said quickly. "I'm not sure if I'll be allowed to." Then she went into the changing rooms and started to get changed.

"She didn't seem very friendly," Poppy said to KC. "She didn't seem to want to talk to us."

KC shrugged. "She's new. Maybe she's a bit shy."

"Well, she won't make many friends if she's going to be like that to everyone," Poppy said.

The week seemed to crawl by. Each day at school, everyone was talking about the disco. They all chose partners to dance with, or made the decision to dance alone. Lots of people asked Paulina if she would dance with them, but she refused.

Poppy noticed that Shantaê didn't take part in

the discussions about the disco, either.

"Maybe they're planning a secret dance routine together," she suggested to KC. "Maybe that's why neither of them wants to dance with anyone else."

KC looked over to where Shantaê was leaning against the wall. She was looking at something she had taken out of her bag and wasn't taking any notice of the girls who were talking excitedly or dancing around.

"Hey, let's go talk to her," KC said to Poppy, and dragged her by the arm across the playground to where Shantaê was standing. When she saw them coming, she stuffed the thing she'd been holding into the front pocket of her bag.

"You OK, Shantaê?" KC asked her. "Are you going to the disco on Saturday?"

"Hi, KC. I guess so. Are you going?"

"Of course we are!" burst out Poppy. "Everyone's going! But you don't seem very excited."

Shantaê shrugged. "Don't suppose I'll win", she said.

Poppy and KC looked at each other.

"Of course you will," said KC. "You're definitely the best dancer in the school. Who else would win? We're really only going along for fun – we won't win."

"Paulina's pretty good," said Shantaê.

"But she's not as good as you," KC replied. The bell went before Shantaê had a chance to say anything. Shantaê picked up her bag.

"See you later," she said, and walked off.

Poppy and KC looked at each other.

"That was pretty strange," said Poppy. "What do you think is going on? She loves dancing – why doesn't she want to go?" They stood watching as Shantaê went around the corner of the building.

"Look!" said Poppy suddenly. "There's Paulina following her! Shall we go and see what they're doing?"

"What do you mean, spy on them? Why? That's not very nice."

"But it's a mystery," Poppy answered. "I'd like

to know if they're going to do a dance routine together."

"I know we love solving mysteries, but this isn't a mystery. They're allowed to plan a routine in secret if they want to – it doesn't need solving! You're just being nosey." And KC poked Poppy in the ribs, gently. But they watched as the two girls came back and headed off in different directions. Now Paulina was putting something in her bag – it looked like the same thing that Shantaê had been looking at. It was thin and square, but Poppy couldn't see what it was, and then it was gone.

The next day was Thursday and they weren't allowed in the school hall because Mr Bass, the caretaker, was getting it ready for the disco. They had an extra-long morning break instead of assembly. As Poppy and KC walked over to the climbing frame, they saw Shantaê and Paulina together again. Poppy nudged KC.

"Look, she's just given something to Paulina again. What do you think it was? It was a square thing – like she had yesterday."

"Don't be so nosey!" said KC.

"But she doesn't look happy, not at all. And look!"

Just at that moment, they saw Paulina grab Shantaê's arm. Paulina was a head taller than Shantaê and seemed to loom over her.

"Shantaê looks frightened," said Poppy. "I'm worried about her. It's not like her to be so quiet and sullen. Usually, she'd be bouncing around the playground with everyone else. Especially if she had a chance to dance! But you would think she didn't even want to go – she hasn't mentioned her dance or said anything about choosing a song."

It was true. Shantaê wasn't acting like herself at all. Even though KC had thought Poppy just wanted it to be mysterious and exciting, she was beginning to think Poppy was right. Maybe something really was going on.

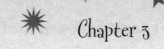

Chapter 3

The Day of the Disco

At last it was Friday. The playground was buzzing – everyone was so excited. At the end of school, a big van drew up and parked outside the gate. Technicians carried sound equipment and reels of cable into the hall and everyone was told they had to keep out of the way – but to be back on time at six o'clock for the start of the disco.

Poppy, KC and Sam went to KC's house first to pick up her outfit for the disco. Then they went to Poppy and Sam's house for some food. Poppy and KC were so excited they could hardly eat anything. Sam grabbed their plates and finished off their food as well as his own.

"Sam, you'll get enormous if you eat so much!" said Poppy. Sam shrugged and took another bite. "Whatever," he said.

But Poppy was glad she didn't have to eat it herself. "I suppose you're not going to dance, though, are you?"

Sam shook his head; his mouth was too full to answer. When he'd finished he said,

"But Emily said I could help with the lighting, so I'm coming along. It will be great, watching you all prancing around."

"Ignore him," said Poppy. "Let's go get ready."

The two girls ran up to Poppy's room and put on the outfits they'd chosen. Then they helped each other with their hair. KC's mum had braided her hair for her the night before. The beads looked fantastic, and their colours matched her outfit. KC helped Poppy to arrange her jet-black hair with lots of sparkly flower clips, and then she sprayed silver hair glitter all over it.

"You look great!" KC said,

"You'll really sparkle in the disco lighting!"

It was still only half past five, but they didn't want to be late. When they'd gone upstairs, Sam was playing on the computer and hadn't changed out of his school clothes. Now, he was nowhere to be seen and the girls were keen to go. Poppy asked her mum if she knew where he was.

"I think he went outside. Shantaê came to the door – she wanted to talk to him."

"Shantaê? What would Shantaê want with Sam?" wondered Poppy.

Sam came through the door, stuffing something into his pocket. Before Poppy could call out to him to ask what was going on, their mum sent Sam straight upstairs to change and wash his face before going out.

When they got to school, there was a big crowd of children waiting outside the hall. They waited until Mrs. Clarke opened the door – then they all tried to rush in together.

"Be careful!" called Mrs. Clarke. "We don't want any accidents before we've even begun! Stop running! I need you each to take a badge with a number on it if you want to be in the dance competition."

That stopped people running – no one wanted to miss out on the competition because they didn't have a badge. Poppy took two badges, handing one to KC. They were numbers twenty-three and twenty-four.

"If you're dancing together, you need to write both numbers down on this sheet," said Mrs. Clarke.

Poppy wrote down both numbers.

"I'm so glad we're dancing together," whispered Poppy to KC. "I'd be too scared to do it on my own."

KC squeezed her hand. "Me too," she said.

The hall looked wonderful. There were pools of red and blue and green light, mirrored balls hanging from the ceiling, and even some special spotlights moving over the crowd that made white clothes glow! On the stage, a boy called Adam was operating the disco. His little sister Emily was on stage, too, in her wheelchair. Emily was in KC and Poppy's class. She was doing the lighting, and she'd told Sam he could help her, as long as he did exactly as she said. So Sam was allowed on stage, where he had a great view of everything. He was very pleased and felt really important.

"Look!" said KC suddenly. She pointed over to a corner of the hall. Mrs. Clarke was talking to a young, woman with long black hair in a plait. The woman held a clipboard and had a microphone pinned to her jacket. "Do you think that's the producer?"

A moment later, the music stopped and Mrs. Clarke walked up the steps onto the stage.

"Welcome to our disco, everyone. As you know, there's something rather special about tonight. This is Miss. Fidah from Network TV. She's a TV producer. And she's here tonight to find the best dancer in the school. The winner will be offered a part in her new TV series, 'The Towers of Moffat Island'."

Miss Fidah smiled and waved to everyone. "Anyone who wants to take part must have a number badge," continued Mrs. Clarke. "See me if you haven't got a badge yet."

"We'll start watching your individual routines in an hour, so make sure you've given your music to Adam on the stage. And make sure we can see your badge clearly. Now, time to get dancing!"

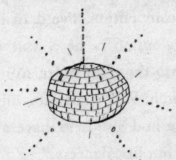

As Mrs. Clarke stepped off the stage, the music started up and the lights flashed around. All the children cheered and then started dancing for all they were worth. They danced non-stop for an hour; no-one dared to rest in case Miss Fidah missed their best moves! Meanwhile, Miss Fidah walked around the dance floor. Every now and then, she peered at someone's number badge and make a note on her clipboard. She stood and watched Poppy and KC for a minute and then wrote their numbers down.

Just when Poppy thought she couldn't dance any more and was about to collapse with exhaustion, Mrs. Clarke and Miss Fidah climbed onto the stage again. Adam turned the music off. This time, Miss Fidah spoke:

"Hello, everybody. I can see there are some really brilliant dancers here. It's now time for the main part of the competition. I've drawn up a random list of badge numbers here, and Adam's sorted the music into the right order, so it should all go without a hitch. We'll start off straight away with numbers five and six. Let's have a big round of applause for our first dancers!"

Everyone clapped and made space as two girls nervously stepped into the middle of the hall. They were from the year above Poppy and KC. As the girls started to dance, everyone cheered. Mrs. Clarke looked pleased. Everyone was enjoying themselves and, even though they all wanted to win, they were all encouraging each other as well. The dancing girls were really very good.

Next was a single dancer, Faith Williams. Poppy didn't know her very well – she was in the year below them. Faith was a tall, fair-haired girl. She didn't dance well at all. Her arms and legs didn't seem to go where she wanted them to and she had no sense of rhythm – she kept getting out of time with the music. But everyone cheered and clapped for her, and she was still smiling when she finished.

Third on the dance floor was another pair from the year above Poppy. They were Miriam and Sadia and they'd chosen an Urdu song. It was completely different from all the other songs Adam had played, and their dance was fantastic. Poppy noticed Miss Fidah smiling and making a note on her clipboard.

Part way through their song, though, all the main lights came on. Mrs. Clarke rushed over to the switch by the door and turned them off again. The poor girls were completely thrown by the accident and they didn't get back into their routine very well at all. Still, everyone clapped and cheered, and they were all sure that Miss Fidah would take the girls' bad luck into account.

On the stage, Adam was signalling wildly at Emily, who was pointing at something on the table. But Poppy and KC didn't have time to watch them for long. The next dancer was number eleven, Paulina.

Poppy and KC were surprised to see that she wasn't doing a routine with Shantaê after all – she really was dancing on her own.

Paulina's routine went without a hitch. It was perfect. She was in time with the music for every step and her routine was polished and energetic. When she finished, she was smiling broadly. She obviously knew it had gone well – and that she must be winning so far.

"That was pretty good," said Poppy. "But I bet Shantaê still beats her. Shantaê's amazing – and there's always a spark to her dancing."

KC nodded in agreement. But there was no time to answer – Miss Fidah was calling out the next numbers: twenty-three and twenty-four. It was their turn! Poppy was shaking with nerves, but KC pulled her on to the dance floor.

"Don't worry," she whispered. "We know we aren't going to win anyway, so there's nothing to be scared about, is there?"

It was true – it wasn't worth being nervous. It would be hard for anyone to beat Paulina – except Shantaê, of course. They danced well together, until KC caught sight of Paulina's stripy jumper as she sneaked across the back of the hall. But how could she be out there? She'd only just left the dance floor! Distracted, KC made a big leap to the left instead of the right, crashing into Poppy. They both sprawled on the floor. Then Poppy laughed. "No point being nervous now!" she said, helping KC up. They managed to finish their number, then fell into each other's arms, giggling.

"Thank you, girls," said Miss Fidah. "Don't

worry about that little slip up. It's hard dancing with a partner! Next is number three."

Chapter 4

Unlucky Number Three

Number three was Benji from Poppy and KC's class. The children standing around him pushed him onto the dance floor, but he was waving his arms around and didn't want to go. Miss Fidah looked puzzled and spoke quietly to Mrs. Clarke.

"I bet they didn't want a boy to play the part," whispered KC to Poppy. But Benji looked as confused as anyone. "Look, he's scared. Poor thing, he's changed his mind. All the other dancers have been girls. He probably didn't know."

"I didn't want to dance," he shouted over the music. But Miss Fidah hadn't heard him. He jiggled around a bit, and everyone clapped, but he obviously didn't have a routine worked out. After half a minute, Miss Fidah came back onto the stage and waved at Adam to turn the music off. She looked embarrassed.

"I'm so sorry about that. And thank you, Benji, for being a good sport. Number three should really be Shantaê, but her badge somehow got stuck on Benji, so let's do that one again." Benji peeled the badge off his t-shirt and slapped it onto Shantaê as she went past him.

"That was bad luck," whispered Poppy.

Shantaê moved into the space in the middle of the hall and waited for the music to start. She looked glum. When it started up, it was the wrong music. Shantaê tried to dance, but her routine didn't match the music. She stood still. After a few seconds, Miss Fidah realised what had happened and raised her hand to get Adam to stop the music again.

"Sorry, Adam, you just played the next song! Shantaê needs the song we've just had for Benji. Can we go back to that song, please?"

Shantaê didn't dance well. People were looking fidgety. They'd just heard this song once, and it was one no one liked. Poppy was rather surprised that Shantaê had even chosen the song as she knew it was by a band that Shantaê hated – and that everyone else hated, too. And then part way through, the music went wrong. It jumped a few bars forwards, stopped briefly, then jumped again. Then it went silent for a couple of seconds. Shantaê tried to carry on dancing through the silence, then stood still. The music picked up again, from a few bars before the point where it had stopped. Poppy looked up at the stage. Adam was gesturing at Sam, who was looking very unhappy. When the song finally came to an end, Shantaê ran off the dance floor pushing through the clouds and headed out to the corridor.

"Poor Taê," said Poppy. "She should have won, but she's not going to now. Why on earth did she pick that song? It's not even any good. And whatever happened to it?"

KC was looking towards the door that Shantaê had gone through.

"Do you think we should follow her?" she tried to say to Poppy, but the music had started up again for the next pair of dancers. And Poppy wasn't taking any notice. She was worried about Sam. Why was Adam cross with him? Surely Sam couldn't have messed up the music; he was only doing light switches.

Next on the dance floor were the twins from

Poppy's class. They were very nervous – so many things had gone wrong in the last few minutes. Miss Fidah watched them carefully but, even though nothing disastrous happened, they clearly weren't going to win. Everyone clapped them, and the twins were perfectly happy at the end of their dance. They loved doing things together, but they were obviously just really glad it was over.

The rest of the dancers came on, mostly in pairs, and did their routines without any more problems. At the very end, Miss Fidah came back onto the stage. The pounding music stopped and Poppy felt her ears buzzing.

"Thank you, everyone – you're all super dancers and I wish there was a part for everyone in the series. It's going to be very hard to decide who has won. I'll leave you to dance while I work out the results and I'll talk to you all again very soon!"

Miss Fidah jumped off the stage and went over to Mrs. Clarke. The two of them went out into the corridor. The music started up and everyone danced again. It was even more fun now they didn't have to worry about dancing their best.

Poppy felt she was dancing much better now she wasn't being watched. Poppy sneaked a look at Sam. He looked a lot happier now the competition was over, too.

They all danced for ten minutes and then Adam turned the music down low for Miss Fidah to announce the winner of the competition. The children were all standing around in groups, holding on to each other – they could hardly wait, and at the same time they didn't want to hear the result! Poppy glanced over to where Shantaê was standing; she looked nervous.

Miss Fidah climbed the stairs to the stage. She went to speak to Adam, who didn't seem happy. He waved his arms around and pointed at an empty space on the desk.

"Well, you were all such fantastic dancers, judging was really difficult. We have three finalists and before I make my very final choice, I'd like them each to dance again. Our finalists are: numbers five and six; number eleven and number three! Please welcome back to the dance floor –"

At that point, Adam walked over and whispered something to Miss Fidah. She nodded and then carried on.

"We have a slight change of plan," said Miss Fidah. "This time, Adam will pick the songs at random and the dancers will have to improvise. I know it's a bit scary, but you're all so good you'll be able to cope. And remember – having fun is the most important thing!"

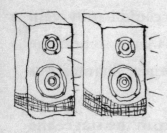

Dancers five and six nervously came out onto the dance floor and Adam played a fast and loud rock track. The dancers jumped and twirled and only bumped into each other once. Everyone cheered and clapped. Next it was Paulina's turn. She was even better. The applause for Paulina was louder still.

Poppy and KC couldn't wait to see what Shantaê would do. But where was she? They looked

around for her. Miss
Fidah announced
twice that it
was her turn.
Then Poppy
saw her slipping
in between people
at the back of
the crowd, coming
towards the dance floor

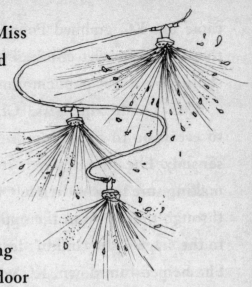

But at the very same moment, the music was
drowned out by the wail of the fire alarm, and
water came cascading from the sprinkler system
in the ceiling onto the dancers below. Everyone
screamed and held their arms over their heads, but
they were all drenched in seconds. It was chaos.
Girls and boys were pushing each other out of the
way as they rushed towards the door, and some
people were slipping on the wet floor. One of the
technicians hit the mains switch to turn all the
electrical equipment off to stop the water ruining
it. The disco lighting went off instantly and for
a moment it was dark until the emergency lights

came on. KC grabbed Poppy's arm — she hated the dark. The wet children were panicking and shouting — it was pandemonium.

Miss Fidah and Mrs. Clarke both shouted to everyone to be calm and leave carefully and sensibly. The other teachers stood by the fire door, making sure the children left safely. Poppy pushed through the crowd in the opposite direction, over to the stage — she couldn't leave Sam on his own! She helped him down. KC was right behind her. She helped Adam push Emily's wheelchair down the ramp. In a few minutes, everyone was outside in the playground and Mrs. Clarke was counting heads to make sure that everyone was outside safely.

The children were starting to shiver in their wet clothes, but they were all chattering excitedly. Mr. Bass the caretaker came out of the building and spoke to Mrs. Clarke, who then blew a whistle to get them all to be quiet.

"OK, everyone, excitement's over. There isn't a fire. There seems to be a problem with the sprinkler system, and when the sprinkler goes off, the fire alarm sounds automatically. But the floor's all wet now, so we won't be able to go back inside and finish dancing, I'm afraid – it would be dangerous. I can see parents turning up to take you all home, so here's Miss Fidah to say a last few words to you."

Miss Fidah stood on tiptoe so that everyone could see her.

"Thank you, everyone, for making this such a fantastic disco and such a hard competition to judge. I hope you enjoyed the unscheduled bit of excitement at the end!" Everyone laughed.

"I'm really sorry that we couldn't see number three's last dance, so I won't take account of the final dances – but we really enjoyed watching them. It's very hard to choose one dancer from all of you – you were all brilliant. But I have to choose just one and that one is: number eleven!"

Paulina's face broke into a huge grin and she went bright red. Poppy looked across at Shantaê again. She was one of the first to step forward and congratulate Paulina. Paulina was delighted.

"It's a shame she doesn't really have any friends

to share it with," said KC, quietly. Poppy thought about it and agreed. "It's always best if you have someone to share good things with."

Shantaê was still standing near Paulina and smiling as people congratulated her.

"Shantaê's so nice," said KC. "She must be disappointed, but she's being really kind to Paulina."

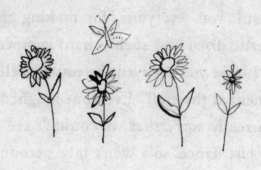

Chapter 5

A Mystery after All

The next morning, Sam was up early and was using the computer when Poppy came downstairs.

"Hey, Sam," she said, rubbing her eyes. "I meant to ask you yesterday. When Shantaê's music went wrong, you were looking really unhappy and it looked like Adam was telling you off. What happened?"

"I don't know," he said. "I was just trying to find out."

"What, on the computer? How are you going to find out on the computer?"

"That song that Shantaê danced to, it's by the Ravin' Ravens, isn't it?"

"Yes. And it's rubbish. Quite apart from it being rubbish, it was totally messed up."

"I know. And that messed-up version is on the internet. I've heard it before. It's in a video about the music industry. It's on this website. Listen."

Sam played the track. It was exactly the same as the messed-up version played at the disco. It ran for a minute or so, then skipped a bit. Then it stopped and went completely quiet. Then it started again, but from a few bars before the point where it had stopped.

"How did you find this, Sam?"

"We did it in music club the other day with Mr Henderson. He showed us the video because we'd had to start our song again lots of times and someone said, "Wouldn't it be awful, if you were in a band, and you had to keep doing your song again and again when you were recording it?" He showed us how people don't have to do that. In a real recording session, they can stop and start and stick the bits together."

"That's great, Sam. But you still haven't said why Adam was cross with you?"

"He thought I messed up."

"But how could you have messed up the music? You were only doing the lights with Emily."

"Because I gave him the track for Shantaê's dance. She came round when you and KC were getting ready and doing your make-up or whatever you were doing up there for about a year and a half. And Adam thought I must have given him the wrong track. But I didn't, honestly, I just gave him what Shantaê gave me."

Poppy thought it was rather strange. Shantaê wouldn't have given him the wrong music – but if she did, she would have given him completely the wrong track, not a mixed-up version from the internet. She wouldn't even have had a mixed-up version.

"I'm going to call KC," she said. "I think there could be a mystery here after all!"

KC had only just got up, but she was pleased to hear from Poppy. She was even happier when she heard there might be a mystery to solve – she loved mysteries just as much as Poppy did.

"That is pretty strange," she agreed. "I wonder how that song could have got there? In fact, the whole disco was pretty messed up, really. I mean, the music, the lights, Benji having to dance – and then the sprinklers! What do you think happened?"

"I don't know. But I'm beginning to think it might be something interesting," said Poppy. "Shall we meet up to work it all out? Can you come over to my house?"

KC's mum was happy for her to go over to Poppy's house, and suggested KC stay all day, if she wanted. That suited KC – she loved spending the day with Poppy and Sam.

To get to Poppy's house, KC had to go past the school. The TV van was still there, and Miss Fidah was showing Mr. Bass something.

"Hi, Mr. Bass," called KC. She hoped he would call her over so that she had an excuse to look inside the TV van at the equipment. She was in luck.

"Hey, KC!" he called. "You might be able to help. Miss Fidah found this jumper on the stage. Do you know whose it is?"

KC ran across the playground and took the striped jumper from Mr. Bass. She did recognise it. She had seen Paulina wearing it when she arrived at the disco. KC had noticed it because it was stripy and nice. KC offered to take it to Paulina's house and Mr. Bass took her to the office to look up Paulina's address.

"I'll see you on Monday, Gordon," Miss Fidah said to the caretaker as she headed back to the hall. "We need to arrange some slots for filming during the holidays."

"They were very impressed by our hall," Mr. Bass told KC. "Now they want to film some of the TV series here. But don't tell anyone yet – it's going to be a surprise!"

Paulina's house was a bit further than Poppy and Sam's house, so KC decided they could return the jumper to Paulina later on.

Poppy was waiting for KC with two mugs of hot chocolate and a plate of biscuits. The two girls took them upstairs to Poppy's room. KC threw Paulina's jumper onto the bed.

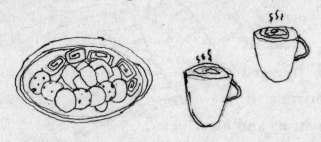

"Is this new?" asked Poppy. "It's really nice. But haven't I seen one like it before?"

"Well noticed," smiled KC. "You make a great detective. Yes, it's Paulina's. She left it behind after the disco. Mr. Bass gave it to me to take to her house. Funny thing is, she left it on the stage, not in the cloakroom. No one was allowed on the stage except Adam, Emily and Sam."

"Yeah, I saw," piped up Sam, who'd just come through the door.

"But she wasn't supposed to be on the stage,"

said Poppy. Sam shrugged. "Whatever," he said as he plonked himself down on Poppy's bed and grabbed a biscuit.

"You said Shantaê was going to win," said Sam.

"We thought she would. But she was unlucky, I guess," said Poppy.

"Like, very unlucky," remarked Sam, taking yet another biscuit.

"Hey," those are our biscuits! Get some of your own!" Poppy snatched the plate away from him.

"What do you mean, Sam?" asked KC.

"Well," Sam mumbled through a mouthful of biscuit. "The whole disco was pretty unlucky. But most things went wrong for her."

"He's right," said Poppy. "If you think about it, things kept on going wrong and they were mostly around Shantaê. That boy, Benji, somehow got her badge and had to dance to her track." Poppy giggled as she remembered Benji jiggling around when he didn't want to dance at all.

"Yes, and her music got mixed up with that

other track, and the sprinkler came on when it was her turn to dance," added KC. "It's like it was jinxed."

"What's jinxed?" asked Sam.

"Or sabotaged," added Poppy.

"What's sabotaged?"

"Jinxed is when something is doomed to go wrong," said KC.

"And sabotaged is when someone has deliberately made it go wrong," added Poppy.

"Why would someone sabotage a disco?" asked Sam.

"Well," Poppy said slowly, as she was thinking out loud. "This disco wasn't only a disco, was it? And as far as I remember, the first part wasn't mixed up at all. Only the competition."

"And the last part," added Sam. "When they were going to dance again. That was jinxed or sabotaged, too." Both girls looked at Sam.

"No it wasn't, Sam," said Poppy. "Nothing happened."

"It did. Or it tried to. Something tried to happen."

KC smiled.

"What tried to happen, Sam?"

"The music disappeared."

"When did that happen?" Poppy asked. "I don't remember the music going off."

"It didn't go off. It disappeared. When they were talking about doing some of the competition again," said Sam.

The two girls were puzzled; they hadn't known anything about this.

"They were going to let some people do their dances again – and they asked Adam to find all the tracks, but all the CDs had vanished. He found them later - when the sprinklers came on - they were all on the floor. It's like they just got there on their own. Do you think it was a lynx?"

"A jinx, Sam, not a lynx. A lynx is like a mountain lion. No, I think it was more likely sabotaged," said Poppy.

"Well," said KC, taking the last biscuit. "If

it was sabotaged, we've got to find out who sabotaged it and why. We're going to need your help, Sam, because you know most about the equipment that was on the stage. You were there all the time. You'll have to try hard to remember everyone who came anywhere the near the stage and anything that you think went wrong."

"The only people on the stage," began Sam, thinking hard, "were Emily and I working the lights, and Adam doing the music. There was also and Mrs. Clarke and Miss Fidah. Oh, and an electrician from the TV crew. I kept seeing him coming on to check things and fiddling with the wires."

"There's no reason an electrician would want to sabotage the disco, is there?" asked KC, feeling confused.

"I can't see any reason," admitted Poppy. "But it's best not to rule out any leads until we have more information. Who else might want to sabotage it?"

"Someone who wanted to win, I suppose," said KC.

"Someone who did win?" suggested Sam. They had all been thinking it, but no one liked to say it. KC fidgeted uncomfortably on the bed.

"We can't jump to conclusions. The TV crew is still at the school. Do you think we should go and talk to the electrician? Sam, you could pretend you left your jacket behind and ask if you could take a look on stage. Just in case there are any clues."

"Whatever," Sam shrugged.

"Good idea," said Poppy. "Let's go and ask my mum if we can go to the school."

Poppy picked up the jumper off the bed.

"Don't forget this," she said. "We can drop it round to Paulina at the same time."

Poppy's mum was happy for them to go out.

"The fresh air will be good for you," she said. "And you can take Jasper for a walk at the same time. Here's his lead."

Jasper pricked up his ears when he heard his name mentioned, and bounded over to the three children. He was always eager to go for a walk, especially when he sensed excitement in the air.

Chapter 6

Another Dancer?

Luckily, the TV crew were still at school. Mr. Bass let them all in to look for Sam's jacket and they went straight to the hall. They had to tie Jasper up outside because he wasn't allowed in the school buildings. Several men stood around, talking about how to make the hall ready for a film shoot. The water was all gone. Sam nudged Poppy and said quietly,

"That one, the one with the beard, he was the one on the stage last night poking around at everything."

The electrician looked up and caught sight of Sam.

"Hello there, Sam. You did a great job of lighting last night. You could get a job on our crew when you're a bit bigger."

Sam was pleased the electrician was impressed. The man turned to Poppy and KC.

"And were you two dancing last night? I've a

daughter your age. She'd have loved to be in that TV series, she adores dancing. She can dance like – well, better than anyone I've ever seen."

"Did she dance last night?" KC asked.

"No," the man said. "My Leanne's out of a job this time. Hamida – Miss Fidah – she wants someone from the school."

Poppy and KC didn't really know what to say.

"Next time," he continued. "What are you here for, anyway? So keen to come back to school you couldn't wait till Monday?"

"I think I left my jacket," said Sam and he darted through the wires and tripods to look under the table. Poppy and KC jumped up onto the stage and pretended to look behind the speakers.

"No, not here," Sam said cheerfully. "I probably left it at home."

They all stood together in the playground. Jasper, pleased to be untied, bounced around and jumped up at Sam to lick his face.

"What do you think?" said Poppy. "He sounded annoyed his daughter couldn't dance in the TV show. Could he have tried to sabotage the disco so that no one from the school got the part?"

"Well," said KC, thinking. "He was on and off the stage, Sam says, so he would have had plenty of chances. And Mr. Bass might have showed him the sprinkler system at the start – he's always careful to make sure anyone using the hall knows all about the fire drill and the equipment."

"We can't just accuse him," said Poppy. "Perhaps we should tell Mr. Bass on Monday." They walked down the road, back towards the house.

"Oh look! We've still got Paulina's jumper here," said Poppy. "I'd forgotten about it. Let's take it back to her now – it's not much past our house and we can still get back in time for tea." She moved the jumper to her other arm and, when she did, something fell out of the pocket.

"Hey, what's that?" she said, bending down to see what had fallen out. "It's a screwed up piece of paper – and it looks like there's something written on it. I wonder what it is?"

She uncrumpled the paper and spread it out. They all peered at it. It seemed to be some kind of a plan.

"I know!" said Sam excitedly. "It's a plan of the hall and the things on the stage. Look – that's the desk where Adam was doing the music. And that's where the lighting controls were on the other table, where I sat with Emily. But I don't know what this bit is. It's a rectangle with numbers on it and one of the numbers is circled in red – number 4."

"Looks like it could be a clue!" said Poppy excitedly.

"Let's take a look at the stage on Monday," said KC. "We can't go straight back to the school now." She put the piece of paper in her own pocket.

Paulina's house was small and very neat-looking with a trimmed lawn. They rang the door-bell and waited. Paulina eventually came to the door; she used the security chain to check who they were before opening it.

"Hi, you guys! No one comes to see me – this is nice! Come in – but please take your shoes off. My mum's fussy about dirt." She looked hard at Jasper.

"Tie him to that tree, over there Sam," Poppy whispered.

Poppy wondered whether it was wise to let Sam in at all. As usual, he was smeared with various types of dirt. She whispered to him not to touch anything, and to keep his dirty hands hidden in his pockets.

Paulina noticed and smiled at him.

"Don't worry," she said. "My mum won't see Sam. She's busy right now."

"We can't stay," said KC. "But we've got your jumper here. You left it behind after the disco on Friday."

Paulina took the jumper. "Thank you!" she said. KC noticed that she didn't check the pocket. Maybe she'd forgotten there was anything in there.

"Well done for winning the competition. You must be really excited!" added Poppy.

Paulina looked pleased.

"Yes, it's brilliant," she said. Then her smile faded a little. "I never thought I'd win. I think Shantaê is supposed to be a really good dancer — everyone thought she'd win. I feel really bad for her. Do you think she minds a lot?"

"I don't know, I haven't seen her," said KC. "She seemed OK on Friday night, didn't she?"

"I'd ask you to stay for some tea —" Paulina began.

"No, don't worry," said Poppy quickly. "We have to get home. My mum will be getting us tea. We just wanted to return you the jumper, in case you were missing it"

"Well, thank you for bringing it over. And now you know where I live, maybe you could come another day?" she sounded hopeful. Poppy felt sorry for her.

As the door closed and they walked away up the street, she said, "She's probably lonely. Maybe she did fix the contest, but I still feel sorry for her not having anyone to see and do things with at the weekend. It can't be nice," said KC.

"Fixing a competition isn't nice, either," said Poppy.

"We don't know that she did it," KC reminded her.

"Well, we'll just have to find out," said Poppy firmly.

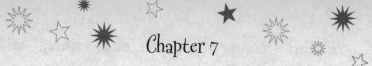

Chapter 7

Time to Investigate

At school on Monday, everyone was talking about the disco and about the dance competition. Paulina was suddenly very popular – everyone wanted to talk to her and ask when she was going to start filming the TV series. But a few girls stood on the sidelines and didn't join in. KC crouched down near them to re-tie her shoelaces, trying to overhear what they were saying without looking too obvious. Then she reported back to Poppy.

"There are definitely some people who think that it wasn't fair – that Shantaê should have won. We'd better try to solve this mystery before it gets nasty."

Poppy smiled and high-fived KC:

"OK, it'll be great to have a mystery to solve again!"

Next lesson was music. They were preparing a song for the end of term play and Mr. Henderson asked for a volunteer to sing a solo. Shantaê put her hand up.

KC looked at Poppy and raised her eyebrows. It wasn't like Shantaê to volunteer for something – she was usually quite shy. Mr. Henderson seemed surprised, too.

"You can certainly try for the solo, Shantaê. You do know that you will have to stand on the stage in front of everyone in the school, and everyone's parents, and sing this song on your own, don't you? Will you be all right doing that?"

"I think so, Sir," said Shantaê.

"OK," Mr. Henderson said. "Let's start off by everyone singing the song together. Then you'll have a chance to learn it and anyone who wants to audition – Shantaê and anyone else – can stay behind today and I'll listen to you doing it on your own."

Shantaê smiled, and looked down at the desk. She went back to drawing on the back of her music book.

"I think I'll have a try," said KC at the end of the lesson.

Poppy looked at her in surprise.

"You? Since when did you like singing?"

"I might just start to like it," she said. "After all, if Shantaê can be brave enough to want to sing in front of everyone, maybe I can, too."

"It's not very nice, to compete against her," said Poppy. "It's not like the disco — we were hopeless at dancing and we were sure she'd win. But what if you're better than her at singing? She'll be disappointed again."

"Don't worry," KC reassured her. "No one in the world is worse at singing than me!"

Poppy waited in the playground. It didn't take long for KC to reappear.

"No go — I'm rubbish. He gave the part to Shantaê. She can really sing!"

"Lucky thing," Poppy said. "She can sing and she can dance. I wish I had a talent."

"You have a talent for solving mysteries," said KC, putting an arm around her friend's shoulder.

"Right! So let's go to your house and do some serious thinking!"

Poppy, KC and Sam sat in the front room while KC's mum looked in the fridge for something interesting for them to eat. "How about milk and toast?"

"That would be lovely, thank you," said Poppy politely.

"We all know what we're thinking," Poppy went on when KC's mum had gone. "We don't like to say it, but all we think Paulina fixed the contest so that she would win. Don't we?"

"Yes," said Sam. "Obviously. She did win. You wouldn't fix a contest and not win – unless you were pretty useless at cheating."

"I'm not sure," said KC. "Don't forget we have two suspects. There's the electrician, too."

KC's mum came back with a plate of toast and glasses of milk. They waited until she had gone before they went on.

"We need to be certain before we accuse either of them," said Poppy through a mouthful of toast. "Let's look at the evidence. Paulina first. She won – but she was the best, so that's not really evidence against her! She had a plan of the stage in her pocket with something circled in red. That's a bit odd, but we can't prove she did anything with it."

"Nothing went wrong with her dance," said KC. "If you think about it, Shantaê's dance went really wrong, but it wasn't just hers."

"Ours went wrong because you fell over, KC," said Poppy.

"I'm really sorry about that," said KC. "But you can't say ours was sabotaged – I just fell over because I was distracted."

"And what distracted you, anyway?"

"Someone moving around at the back of the hall."

"Who?" asked Poppy.

"Um, Paulina. Someone in a striped jumper. A striped jumper like that one we gave back to Paulina."

"Aha! Told you so!" said Sam triumphantly. "She was trying to make you fall over!"

"That's a bit far-fetched," said KC.

"And there were those girls who just couldn't dance together," continued Poppy.

"That's not sabotage either, they just didn't practise," KC said.

"And that girl who went on third. Her dance didn't work either – the main lights came on. Why did that happen, Sam? You were on lights, do you know?"

"Yes," he said. There was a sticky note saying to turn that switch on after 15 seconds in dance three, so Emily did it. The note must have been on the wrong switch. That could have been sabotage, too."

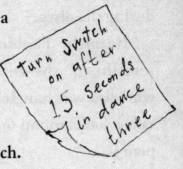

Sam was still certain that Paulina had sabotaged the disco, but KC was sure he was wrong.

"Think about it," she said. "Isn't it clear that whoever won would be the obvious suspect? Especially if nothing went wrong with her routine. Why would she expect to get away with it?"

"Well, maybe she's stupid," suggested Sam.

"Not so stupid," added Poppy "– after all, she did win and no one has contested it."

"I still think you're wrong," said KC.

"Well, do you have any other ideas?" Poppy asked her.

"Apart from that electrician? Not yet. But I will. I just need to think."

Next day, KC asked Sam to introduce her to the electrician who had been hanging around the stage during the disco.

"It might be him. Or he might have seen something," she said. "Or he might have noticed who else was hanging around. And anyway, I can take a look around to find out what that box on the plan is."

They went to the hall in morning break.

"Still looking for your jacket?" asked the electrician, when he saw Sam.

"Um, no, not really," Sam said. Suddenly he couldn't think of a good way of introducing KC. Why would she want to talk to an electrician?

"Hi," said KC, shyly. "I'm KC. I wondered if you could show me how the lighting and stuff works. I'm really interested in – um, stage lighting and sound recording. I'd like to work in TV one day."

"Sure," said the electrician. "What does KC stand for? My name's Kevin Cavendish, so I'm a KC, too!"

"It's just KC," she said. KC never told anyone what her name was. Sam knew there was no point in asking her. Even Poppy didn't know, and she was KC's closest friend.

"All right, then, KC. Come over here and I'll show you what we've got. But we'll have to be quick. You'll have lessons soon and I have to get back to work. I've got to check all this stuff before lunchtime. We start filming some test footage tomorrow."

Kevin showed KC all the equipment and how it worked together.

"Anything else I can show you?" Kevin asked. KC shook her head and thanked him, then went towards the door. On the door was a hand-written sign. It said:

DANGER – SWITCH 4 NOT WORKING

"What's switch 4?" asked KC.

"The sprinkler switch – we've disabled it while we check it. We don't want the sprinkler going off again with all this electrical stuff around."

"Where is it?" asked KC.

"At the side of the stage," said Kevin. "In that box," and he pointed to a metal box on the wall. Why?"

"No reason," said KC and smiled.

Outside, she told Sam that she'd found out what the circled "4" was on the plan and asked him if he'd discovered anything.

"I'm not sure," said Sam.

"What do you mean?" asked KC.

"I'll tell you later," said Sam. "If I'm right."

At the end of school, they all cycled home together and KC went to Poppy and Sam's house. Sam disappeared to the computer immediately. After five minutes he called out to the two girls.

"Hey, come here! You're right! Maybe it wasn't Paulina after all! Look at this!"

They went over to see what he'd found. He showed them a video of a girl dancing.

"Who is it?" asked Poppy

"It's Leanne Cavendish," said Sam smugly.

"Who?" KC and Poppy asked together.

"You weren't taking any notice, were you?" Sam said. "You asked me to introduce you to the electrician, and you weren't taking any notice at all! He's called Kevin Cavendish. And the other day he told you his daughter was called Leanne. And that she wanted to be in the show but she couldn't be. And that Miss Fidah wanted some new talent. Well I recognised the name, because she's in Alien Huntress of the Northern Galaxy so I thought I'd look her up – and here we are! She does lots of TV and she's a dancer too!"

"That's so smart!" said Poppy, and hugged Sam. He squirmed out of the hug quickly. "So you mean the electrician sabotaged the disco because he didn't want anyone else to get the part – so that Miss Fidah would give it to his daughter after all?"

"But it didn't work," said KC. "So now maybe

he'll do something else to sabotage the test filming so that Paulina comes out of it looking rubbish and his daughter still gets the part!"

"So we have to make sure he doesn't get the chance," said KC.

"Just as well you pretended to be interested in the electrics," said Sam. "Now you can ask if you can watch while they do the filming. He won't dare try anything while he's being watched."

They were all feeling satisfied and pleased, especially with Sam's excellent bit of detective work, but then KC thought of something.

"But, hang on a minute," she said. "The plan of the stage was in Paulina's pocket. Why would she have that if the electrician was the one who wanted to mess up the disco?"

"Aaaargh, it's so confusing!" exclaimed Poppy, and put her hand to her head. "To start with it all looked so straight-forward, but now we have two suspects so we'll have to do some serious detective work to sort out what's really going on!"

"We still have the piece of paper,

don't we?" asked KC. "So we can show it to Paulina tomorrow and see if she looks guilty when she realises we know she had that plan."

"Good idea," said Poppy. "And you can ask if you can watch the electrician. At this rate, you'll be qualified to do the electrics yourself, you'll know so much about it!"

"And what can I do?" asked Sam.

"You can find out as much as possible about Leanne Cavendish – we might need that information."

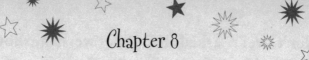

Chapter 8

A Pattern of Threes

The next day, Poppy took the crumpled piece of paper from Paulina's pocket into school. She and KC found Paulina waiting in the playground before school and went over to her. She smiled at them.

"Thanks for bringing my jumper back," she said. "My mum is really grateful. She complains that I'm always losing things. Though it wasn't really my fault I lost that. Where did you find it?"

"You left it on the stage," said Poppy. "But we also found this piece of paper. It was in the pocket but it fell out. I'm sorry, we didn't notice it."

KC and Poppy watched carefully as Paulina unfolded the paper and looked at it.

"What is it?" she asked. "Are you sure it's from my jumper?"

"Well, yes," said Poppy. "We really are sure. Isn't it yours?"

"I've never seen it before," she said "It's a

picture of some kind – but I don't know what it is." She showed it to Poppy and KC. They didn't know what to say.

"I think it's a plan of the stage, at the disco," KC said at last. They both watched Paulina closely, looking for clues. But she seemed genuinely confused.

"I don't know how that would have got into my pocket," she said.

The bell rang and they all had to go into school. Poppy and KC stopped in the cloakroom to compare notes.

"What do you think?" whispered KC.

"She seemed really surprised. So, unless she's a very good actress . . . I don't know what to think."

At lunchtime, KC went to the hall to ask Kevin Cavendish if it would be okay if she watched the recording session in the afternoon.

"Hi, KC," he said. "Shame we can't be KCs together, but I'm afraid I won't be here, then. I'm going to do something with my daughter. Rod here will be doing it tonight," and he pointed out Rod to KC. "He'll let you watch."

KC didn't really need to watch if Kevin wasn't going to be there, but she couldn't see a polite way out.

"Thank you. Oh, Kevin – did you see anyone else go on stage on Friday during the disco – apart from Sam and Adam and Emily, I mean."

"The girl with the striped jumper. That's all," he said. "It's a funny school this – all you girls being interested in how the electrics work!"

"What do you mean?" KC asked him.

"That girl with the striped jumper, she wanted to know how it all works. And now you. It's usually boys who want to see the kit. That's all. But it's good – we need more female electricians!"

"Paulina again," thought KC." It's not looking good for her." She went outside and told Poppy what had happened.

"I've been thinking," said Poppy. "When she said her mum was always telling her off for losing things, she said 'this time it's not really my fault'. What do you think she meant by that?"

"Don't you ever say it's not your fault when you lose something?" said KC. "I do. My mum never accepts it, though. She says, 'It's your responsibility to keep track of your stuff. If you leave it lying around and someone takes it, that's your fault. If you lend it to someone, you have to make sure you get it back'."

The two girls looked at each other – and both started to speak at once.

"What if it wasn't Paulina in the striped jumper?!"

"Yes," Poppy continued. "What if she had put it down and someone else took it. Or if she lent it to someone?"

"Of course! She would have taken it off to dance – it was so hot in there," added KC. "We'll have to ask her after school. Come on, let's go to class before we're in trouble."

At the end of school, Poppy and KC stood outside the school gate waiting for Paulina to appear. But they saw someone else first. They watched a girl with crutches make slow progress over the playground towards the hall.

She didn't seem very sure where she was going.

"She looks familiar," said KC. "But I don't think she goes to our school."

"You're right – I'm sure I've seen her somewhere before," agreed Poppy. The two of them jogged across the playground and caught up with the girl.

"Hi," said Poppy. "You're not from here, are you? We wondered if you needed any help finding something?"

"Oh, that's really nice of you – thank you," the girl smiled at them. "I'm going to the hall. Isn't it through here?"

"Yes," said KC. "Are you part of the filming? That's what they're doing in there tonight. They're making a bit of film for a TV series. It's very exciting. One of our friends is in it."

"I know they're filming – but I'm not in it this time." She picked up one of the crutches and waved it in the air. "I'm out of commission at the moment."

"Sweetheart!" It was Kevin Cavendish, bursting through the door and into the playground. "I was going to meet you at the gate. Am I late? I'm sorry!

Girls, this is my daughter, Leanne. I have to take her to the hospital to the fracture clinic. That's why Rod's doing the recording tonight. Leanne, sweetie, these are two super girls – KC is especially super because she likes electrical equipment and she's called KC!"

Leanne smiled. "I know they're super, they just offered to help me find my way to the hall."

"You're Leanne Cavendish?!" exclaimed Poppy. "That's why we thought we recognised you. My brother showed us your picture. He watches that thing you were in – Alien Huntress of something or other."

"Alien Huntress of the Northern Galaxy. Yes, awful, isn't it? But, as you can see, I'm not doing any work at the moment. I fell out of my spaceship and broke my ankle."

"Really?" asked Poppy.

"No, not really. Nothing so glamorous. I fell

off my bicycle. Got my shoe laces caught in the chain."

"Will you give me your autograph, for my brother, please?" asked Poppy.

"Sure. Have you got a pen?"

Leanne signed her name on a page of Poppy's notebook and then she took hold of Poppy's hand and signed the back of it.

"Ooooh, he'll be so jealous!" cried KC. "That's great."

"Yes, great," said Poppy. "He'll want to cut off my hand!"

"Come on, sweetie, we have to go," said Kevin. "KC, Rod will let you watch if you want to."

Leanne said goodbye to them and left with her dad.

"Well," said Poppy. "That rules them out. He wasn't going to sabotage the disco so she could get the dancing part if she has a broken ankle – in fact, that's probably why there's a dancing part available at all!"

"Yes," agreed KC. "Back to the drawing board!"

Chapter 9

A Surprise Trip

"Hey, Poppy," said Sam, bursting into his sister's bedroom just before bedtime. "Guess what I've found out? She did it herself! Shantaê put the lynx on her song herself."

"Jinx, Sam, the jinx. And, what do you mean, she did it herself?"

"Look. I've still got the CD she gave me with the song on for her dance. Adam gave it to me to give back to her, but I forgot."

"And?"

"And it's the one from the video that's all messed up. But I know she gave it to me because she wrote on the label – look. So no one switched it. And the time stamp for the track is that afternoon – so no-one could have taken it and recorded over it after she gave it to me, or the time stamp would be later, in the evening."

"Nice work, Sam!" Poppy congratulated him. "It's a good thing you're such a genius with the computer! But why would she want to sabotage her own dance routine? It just doesn't make sense."

"Time for bed, you two," Poppy's mother called upstairs. "Whatever mystery you're trying to solve will have to wait until the morning."

"Where did she get that recording from though? How did she even know about it?"

"She's in music club," said Sam. "Didn't I tell you?"

"No, you forgot to mention that little detail."

"Hurry up! Stop gossiping," their mum shouted from the bottom of the stairs.

"We'll tell KC in the morning," Poppy said to Sam. "She'll be impressed – but we'd better go to bed now or we'll be in trouble."

KC was late to school, and then she was whisked away by Mrs. Clarke for the whole day to paint sets for the school play. Poppy didn't get a chance to talk to her at all. By the end of the day, Poppy was almost bursting – she had to tell KC their latest discovery! But, out in the playground, Poppy's mum was waiting for her. Sam was bouncing around her, and Jasper was bouncing around Sam.

"Surprise!" said Poppy's mum. "I'm taking you two for a treat!"

Poppy's heart sank. Although she wanted to know what the treat was, she wanted to talk to KC more than anything else. She could see KC coming out of the other door and walking across the playground towards her.

"Can I just talk to KC, first?" she asked.

"You don't need to – KC's coming with us," said Poppy's mum. "Run and get her."

Poppy's mum hurried them all to the car before the girls had a chance to talk. Fifteen minutes later, they drew up in the car park of the skating rink. They were going ice-skating.

"I thought you might need cheering up after falling over at the disco and missing your chance to be on TV," said Poppy's mum. "Here are your tickets – go and get your skates on! I'll take Jasper for a walk and see you in the café later."

Poppy and KC ran off to the skate-hire booth. Sam stumbled after them – he'd already started to take his shoes off and now he was falling over them. As they sat on the benches clicking the fastenings on their skates, Poppy finally had the chance to tell KC what Sam had discovered.

"So, you mean, Shantaê herself gave Sam the wrong music? On purpose?"

"Looks like it," said Poppy. "Sam says it can't have been switched and it was in his pocket until he gave it to Adam."

"But why would she do that? It must have been a mistake."

They had their skates on now, and moved to the edge of the ice to wait for their turn. The marshals were clearing the last lot of skaters from the rink. At last it was their turn. KC and Poppy hadn't been skating for a while and at first they clung to the sides. Sam was more confident but not a very good skater. He whizzed out on to the ice and bumped straight into someone and landed with a thud on his bottom. The girls laughed and helped him up. Loud disco music started up and they circled the rink, slowly moving further away from the edges. After a few minutes, Poppy and KC were getting into the swing of it and were going faster, weaving between the slower children and even trying to trace figures of eight in the ice. Sam was only interested in going fast. He was so short he could hurtle around like a cannonball. No matter how many times he fell over – and it was a lot – he picked himself up and shot off again. He didn't stop to talk to the girls even once.

Halfway through their session, everyone had to clear the ice while a big machine came on and cleaned the surface. Poppy and KC leaned against the wall watching the machine, while Sam chattered on, talking about how it worked.

KC thrust her hands deep into her pockets to try to warm them up. She hadn't known they were coming skating, so she hadn't got any gloves. Her fingers touched the crumpled up piece of paper with the plan of the stage on it, and she pulled it out to look at it again. As she flattened it out, she saw there was something stuck on the back of it and turned it over.

"What's that?" Poppy asked.

"I'd just noticed it," KC said. "It's a screwed-up sticker. Let me straighten it out. It's a got a number on it – number three. It's one of those stickers from the disco! It must be dancer number three. Who was that?"

They thought for a minute.

"It was Benji," said KC. "Maybe he did it, then!"

"No, Benji didn't even want to be in the disco competition. He wouldn't have had a reason to mess it up."

"Of course, you're right! It was Shantaê's number. Shantaê was number three! And as she went onto the dance floor, he slapped the sticker on her arm!"

"If this was in Paulina's pocket…" said Poppy slowly. "And Paulina wasn't wearing her jumper, then Shantaê must have been wearing it! Which explains how Paulina could have got to the back of the hall so fast – it wasn't her! It was Shantaê, wearing Paulina's jumper."

"And she had the plan of the stage in her pocket with the sprinkler switch marked," added KC. "She must have stuffed the sticker in her pocket and it stuck to the plan. And she asked Kevin to show her the kit on stage, when she was wearing the jumper – because he said it was a girl in a stripy jumper and we assumed it was Paulina. But it was only Paulina's jumper!

"We have to get to the bottom of this," said

Poppy. "Everything leads us back to Shantaê."

It was time to start skating again. KC pushed the piece of paper back into her pocket and they set off, darting between the other skaters and practising turns so fast they sent showers of ice dust into the air, just like snow. On the next circuit, Poppy bumped straight into KC. They fell in a heap on the ice.

"Weren't you looking where you were going?" asked KC. "I thought you were good at this!"

"Sorry," said Poppy, barely pausing for breath, "but I just realised something. Three! There's a pattern of threes here!"

"Where? What are you talking about?"

Poppy held up three icy fingers.

"The mixed-up disco — there's a pattern of threes. Shantaê's badge at the disco was number three. First, the badge got onto Benji and he had to dance. Second, Shantaê got number three back and her music was messed up. Third, Kate and Ellie's routine was messed up because the main lights went on."

"What's that got to do with 'three'?" asked KC.

Other skaters were whizzing past them, swerving to avoid the girls sitting on the ice. Some gave them cross looks and one shouted at them. But Poppy was too excited to take any notice of the shouts.

"They were the third to dance! Don't you remember? Sam said there was a sticky note next to the switches that said "Dance three: turn on after 15 seconds." Emily must have counted the dances instead of waiting for dancer number three. And dancer number three was Shantaê – it was supposed to come on in Shantaê's dance!"

"So who wrote the note? Who has it?"

One of the skating wardens was coming over to see if they were all right.

"I think it will have been thrown away," said Poppy. "But I bet you anything Shantaê wrote it. And I bet she put her number three sticker on Benji, too."

"Come on, up you get," KC said. "That guy's

going to be here in a moment. But I bet you're right. Why would Shantaê sabotage her own dance routine?"

Soon it was the end of the hour and the three of them, exhausted and covered in powdered ice, piled back into the changing area to take off their skates.

Chapter 10

An Expert Skater

"You were pretty good – I saw those turns!" said a voice from behind KC and Poppy. KC spun round – it was Shantaê! She had a pair of blue skates dangling from her hand. They weren't the hire skates like they'd been wearing, but professional skates instead.

"I didn't know you skated!" said Poppy.

"Ice dancing," Shantaê replied. "My mum wants me to do it. I don't mind; it's fun. I have a class now. You can stay and watch if you like."

"We'd love to," said KC. "Poppy's mum is waiting for us, though. But Shantaê - this might sound strange. We were wondering if you had borrowed Paulina's jumper the other night at the disco?"

"Well, yes, I was cold. And she said I could. Oh no – I didn't give it back, did I? I'd completely forgotten. What shall I do? Is it lost?"

"No, don't worry," said Poppy. "You left it at the

disco. She's got it back now. Miss Fidah found it."

"She's got it back? Good!" But then a look of panic crossed her face. "Do you know where she lives? I think I left something in the pocket."

Poppy and KC looked at each other.

"What sort of something?" asked KC.

"Only a bit of paper," said Shantaê quickly. "Nothing important. It doesn't matter if she throws it away."

"This bit of paper?" asked KC, taking it from her pocket. They both watched Shantaê carefully. She was clearly anxious. She held out her hand to take it, but KC just unfolded it to show it to her. Shantaê's face fell.

"I can explain," she said. "If you promise not to tell anyone. But now I have my skating lesson."

"I think we might just stay and watch," said Poppy. "I'll ask my mum if we can all sit in the café. It will be good to see some proper skating - you can show us how it should really be done."

KC and Poppy sat in the café, warming their hands on steaming mugs of hot chocolate. Sam had orange juice. The frost that had covered Sam so that he looked like a snowman had melted and stood in little beads of water all over his clothes.

At last, Shantaê's class finished and she skated over to the café. Poppy's mum phoned Shantaê's mum to say she'd give Shantaê a lift home, then went off to buy more hot chocolate. Poppy and KC waited for Shantaê's explanation.

"So," said Poppy. "You had the plan to the hall and you marked the sprinkler switch. You set off the sprinkler, I suppose, to put an end to the disco?"

She looked at the floor, miserably.

"I'm so, so sorry," she said. "I really didn't want to mess it up for everyone else. I thought I could fix it just a bit, just to make sure Paulina won – but then they wanted to do the extra bit, to give me another chance!"

Poppy and KC looked at each other in surprise.

"To make sure Paulina won?" asked KC. "Why did you want Paulina to win? Didn't you want to win?"

"No," Shantaê said miserably. "I really didn't

want to win. I knew that it would be a close-run contest between me and Paulina."

"It wouldn't," interrupted KC, "You're much better than Paulina. You know you are. Why did you want her to win? Is that why you messed up your own music?"

Shantaê nodded. "I just wanted her to win. Paulina's new here. She wants to be good at something. She wants to be noticed and to make friends. I thought if she had the TV part people would be interested in her."

"And your number badge – number three. Did you put that on Benji?"

Shantaê nodded again. "I didn't write my name down and I thought I could just lose the sticker and not have to dance. I shouldn't have put it on Benji – that was stupid. The other kids pushed him onto the dance floor and he was scared to leave. I'm sorry about that. Mrs. Clarke must have noticed it was my number when they were going round watching people."

Just then, Poppy's mum came back with the drinks. They didn't want to talk about it in front of her, so they asked Shantaê about her ice dancing lessons. But KC and Poppy were impatient. The mystery was hardly solved – it was getting even more mysterious!

Chapter 11

Friends After All

Poppy and KC met outside the school gate next morning.

"I've been thinking," said Poppy. "I don't really believe what Shantaê said about wanting Paulina to win so she would be popular. Do you remember, the day before the disco, we saw her give something to Paulina, and Paulina grabbed her arm. What do you think was going on? Do you think Paulina has been bullying Shantaê? Maybe she forced her to rig the disco so that she'd win!"

"That's possible," said KC. "But how will we find out? Paulina won't tell us, and Shantaê's not likely to change her story now."

"Unless she thinks we know already," suggested Poppy. "Come on, let's go talk to her."

Shantaê was hanging up her coat. But before Poppy and KC could get to her, Paulina went over. Poppy and KC hung back, fiddling with their bags and watching. This time, Paulina was giving something to Shantaê.

"Thanks for lending me these," she said. "It was really good. I'm sorry it didn't turn out so well for you."

"Oh, no problem," Shantae smiled. "I don't mind at all."

As Paulina went into her classroom down the corridor, Poppy and KC went up to Shantaê. She smiled at them.

"Hello, you two. Thank you for not telling Paulina that I messed up the disco. I really want her to think she won it fairly. And she is a good dancer, she really is. She just needs some lessons, and she'll get them now, because the TV station will pay!"

"Shantaê," Poppy began. "This might sound a bit strange, but is Paulina nice to you? She seems a bit, – well, distant – to most people."

"Oh yes, she's lovely. I really like her. She's just shy. But so am I, so I can understand that."

"I'm shy too, so I know how you feel," added KC.

"I lent her a couple of my CDs because she didn't have any music to dance to – she just gave them back. She was so pleased, it was sweet. And it was a good way of making friends."

"So is that what you were doing?" laughed KC, relieved. "I saw you giving her things, and I wondered if she was bullying you. I was going to tell Mrs. Dean. I'm glad I didn't now."

"Oh no," said Shantaê. "I wanted to lend them to her. I was a bit worried I'd be in trouble, though, because one of them was my brother's. I told her not to tell anyone. But he didn't even notice."

Mrs. Clarke came hurrying down the corridor.

"Come along, girls! Stop gossiping and get into your classroom please!" she said, bustling them in through the door.

After school, Shantaê caught KC as she was leaving.

"Do you want to come and hear the song? I wondered if you'd like to – it's going really well, but I'm still nervous. Do you mind?"

"I'd love to," said KC. "Can Poppy come along, too?"

The three of them went into the hall. Mrs. Coates was already sitting at the piano. Shantaê started to sing the solo. Her voice was beautiful, and she was completely transformed when she started singing. Poppy thought it was even better than watching Shantaê dance. When she danced, all her shyness evaporated. Her singing was just as good – but there was something better. She looked radiant. When she had finished, her cheeks were flushed and she seemed almost electric with energy.

"What do you think?" Shantaê asked excitedly.

"That was fantastic!" said Poppy. "I had no idea you could sing like that."

"Yes, you could be a pro," said an unfamiliar voice behind them. Poppy and KC spun round. It was Miss Fidah, the TV producer. She was standing at the back of the hall, smiling. Slowly, she clapped.

"Well done, number three," she said. Shantaê blushed.

"I didn't know you were there," she said.

"I wasn't," answered Miss Fidah. "I was sorting out some arrangements with Mrs. Clarke and I heard you when I was in the corridor. So I came in to see who it was. Your voice is fantastic. I was wondering… you might not want to do this, and I know you have the school play to rehearse for – but I was wondering if you might like to sing in the TV show? As you know, we have a lot of disco scenes. In one of them, there's a live band. We haven't put the band together yet. But I'd very much like you to be the lead singer. What do you think?"

Shantaê was beside herself with excitement. Poppy and KC jumped up and down – they were so excited too!

"I – yes! Please, yes! That would be fantastic," Shantaê said. "I'd love it, I'd totally love it – thank you SO much!"

The three girls hugged each other, and Miss Fidah laughed.

"Well, I'm sure you will be able to do it easily. And it's not as hard as singing a solo in the school play. On film, you have lots of chances to get it right! If you make a mistake, we can just film it again – so you don't even need to be nervous. I'll need permission from your parents, obviously," said Miss. Fidah. "Is that likely to be a problem do you think?"

"No, no – I don't think so," said Shantaê. "Although – my mum is very disappointed that I didn't get the dancing part." She looked down at the ground for a moment, not sure what to say next.

"Yes, Mrs. Clarke told me you are a very good dancer. She wanted to get you to dance again – she thought you should have won the contest at the disco."

"Oh, I don't mind at all!" said Shantaê. "I'd much rather sing. I don't really want to do so much dancing."

"We have to go," said Poppy suddenly, and she dragged KC by the arm out of the hall. Miss Fidah and Shantaê looked surprised, but not as surprised as KC.

Chapter 12

A Song and Dance

"What was that about?" she asked, when they were outside.

"It was her mum!" said Poppy.

"What was? Her mum mixed up the disco?"

"No, silly. It was her mum who wanted her to win. And she didn't want to. It wasn't that she really wanted Paulina to win, but that she really wanted to lose," said Poppy.

"But why would she want to lose?" KC asked. "It doesn't make any sense."

"Yes, it does. She didn't want to dance on TV. She just said – she'd much rather sing. But her mum wants her to dance."

"But she's a brilliant dancer!" said KC.

"She is – but she doesn't have to do it just because she's good at it. Her mum was a professional dancer – she probably makes Shantaê dance. I bet she's always pushing her, and Shantaê's just got sick of it."

When Shantaê came out Poppy and KC confronted her again.

"Will you tell us what's really going, on?" asked KC. "We know everything you did. You tried to avoid dancing at all; you messed up your music so that you wouldn't win; you tried to get the lights turned on in your routine, but just messed up someone else's dance. When they wanted to do a second round you hid the CDs. And when that didn't work, you set the sprinkler off and ruined the whole disco."

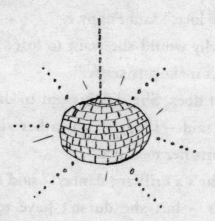

"How did you find out all that?" gasped Shantaê.

"You borrowed Paulina's jumper. And the electrician said the girl with the striped jumper was messing about on the stage. And then you left the jumper behind, and it had the plan of the stage in it, with the sprinkler switch circled. In the beginning we thought that Paulina had messed up the disco so that she would win," said Poppy.

"Oh no!" interrupted Shantaê. "It would have been awful if she had got into trouble for it!"

"But we knew it couldn't have been her," continued Poppy. "She didn't know anything about the plan of the stage - she didn't even know it had been in her pocket. And it had your number three badge on it."

"And we found out she doesn't have a computer," added KC.

"What's that got to do with it?" asked Shantaê.

"The music you gave Sam for your dance - you saved it from the internet. She couldn't have done that."

"There's only one thing we don't know," said Poppy. "If you didn't want to win the competition, why did you bother to enter it? Why spoil it for everyone else? Did your mum force you to enter the competition?"

Shantaê was almost in tears.

"I didn't want to spoil it for anyone, really, I didn't. But I just had to lose. And I knew I couldn't just dance badly or not take part because my mum would know I'd done it on purpose and she would have been so disappointed. Then when Paulina turned out to be a good dancer, and my mum hadn't ever seen her dance, I thought that was the perfect opportunity. Paulina could win and there'd be nothing my mum could do about it, but I wouldn't have to disappoint her.

"I'm really ashamed. I should just have been brave enough to tell my mum I didn't want to dance. But she's worked so hard to pay for my dance classes for years. She really wants me to be a professional dancer, and my dance teacher says it's perfectly possible. That just makes things even worse!"

KC put her arm around Shantaê's shoulder.

"Don't you think," she said gently, "it would be better to tell your mum now than let her carry on spending loads on dance classes you don't want to go to?"

"Oh, it's not that I don't want to go! I love dancing, I really do – but I don't want to be a dancer. I want to be a singer. That's my real dream. But I've never told anyone before. My mum only signed me up for singing lessons because she said I'd have a better chance of getting into dance school. I've never told her how much I love them."

"Well, I think it's time to tell her now. Here she is," Poppy pointed out as Shantaê's mum came into the playground.

"Please stay with me and help me explain," Shantae pleaded. "It won't be as hard with you guys here."

"Of course we will", KC said. "But I don't think it'll be as bad as you think. Things always seem worse if you've been worrying about them. And I'm sure she only wants you to be happy."

"Hi, girls," said Shantaê's mum as she caught up with them all. "How are things? Did you enjoy the disco on Friday? It sounds as though it got rather mixed up, but I hope you managed to have fun."

"Yes, thank you," said Poppy. "Um, we've just been listening to Shantaê sing. She's got the solo in the school musical! And – you tell her, Shantaê."

Shantaê looked awkward and shuffled her feet. He mum spoke before she had a chance to say anything.

"That's great, Taê! Well done! Just as well you've had those singing lessons."

"I really like singing," Shantae blurted out. "I don't mind about the disco, really I don't. I'd rather concentrate on singing. I want to do it really well."

"That's great," smiled her mum. "Your singing teacher is very enthusiastic – she says you have a great voice. She said with a bit of training, you could be a star!"

Shantaê beamed. And then her face fell.

"But I can't be a star singer and a star dancer," she said. "There isn't time to do both. You always told me that to succeed as a dancer I have to put it above everything else."

"Then you have to choose," her mum said. "Which do you really want to do?"

"What, you mean I can choose either one?"

"Of course you can," laughed her mum. "Why not?"

"You're so lucky," KC put in. "I'd love to be able to choose – and I can't do either, I'm hopeless!"

Shantaê looked carefully at her mum. She was still afraid of upsetting her.

"I really, really want to sing," she said at last. "I do love dancing, but I don't want to be a dancer. Not enough to make it work. But I love singing above everything else."

"Then that's settled, then," said her mum. "You can keep on as many dance classes as you like, but you can concentrate on singing."

"And you don't mind?"

"Of course I don't mind! I wanted to give you the chance to be a dancer – I didn't want you to realise too late that you'd missed out. But I never intended to force you to dance. You can do whatever you like!"

Shantaê hugged her mum so hard she almost fell over.

"Thank you, thank you so much!" she exclaimed. "I thought you'd be so disappointed if I didn't want to dance. I needn't have gone to all that trouble. I'm sorry KC, sorry Poppy."

"What trouble? Sorry for what?" asked her mum.

"I think you have a bit of explaining to do," said Poppy. "But we'll leave you to do that – number three," and she winked at Shantaê, then linked arms with KC and they turned to leave.

"Wait!" It was Miss Fidah, coming out of the hall. "I need to arrange a rehearsal with you."

"Rehearsal for what?" asked Shantaê's mum. "Who is this woman?"

"What, all of us?" asked Poppy, surprised. "It's

only Shantaê you need."

"No, change of plan," smiled Miss Fidah. "There were so many good dancers at the disco, and we will need lots of extras, that I've decided you can all be in the crowd scenes. What do you say?"

The three girls leaped up and down and squealed with excitement.

"I think that's a yes," smiled Shantaê's mum.

"And I promise you," said Miss Fidah, "that with my brilliant technical crew, these discos will definitely not get mixed up!"

Three Together

If you've enjoyed meeting Poppy,
KC and Sam, you can try one of these
other exciting books in the
Three Together series.